To Michael, Becky & Isabel

First Edition, September 2022
10 9 8 7 6 5 4 3 2 1
FAC-034274-22217
Printed in the United States of America

This book is set in Century 725/Monotype; Grilled Cheese/Fontbros; Typography of Coop, Fink, Neutraface/House Industries
Reinforced binding

Library of Congress Cataloging-in-Publication Control Number: 2022932407
ISBN 978-1-368-07224-3

Visit www.hyperionbooksforchildren.com and www.pigeonpresents.com

# An ELEPHANT & PIGGIE BIGGIE!

## Volume 5

## By Mo Willems

Hyperion Books for Children / *New York*

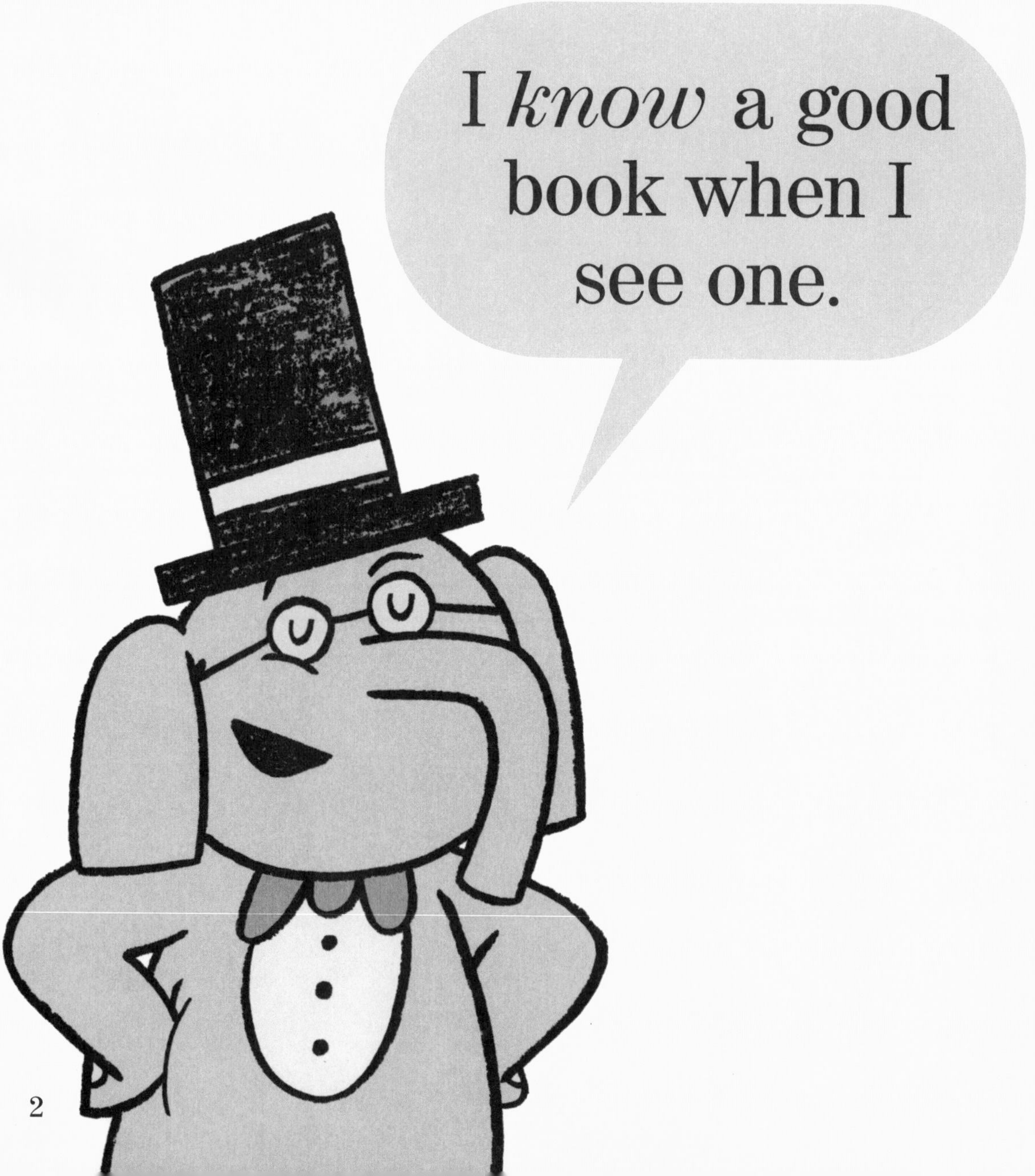
I *know* a good book when I see one.

An **ELEPHANT & PIGGIE** Book

# I Am Invited to a Party!

By **Mo Willems**

Originally published in September 2007.

# I Am Invited to a Party!

An **ELEPHANT & PIGGIE** Book
By **Mo Willems**

Hyperion Books for Children / *New York*

Gerald!

It is cool.

Will you go with me?

I have never been
to a party.

I will go with you.

I *know* parties.

17

Really?

I know parties.

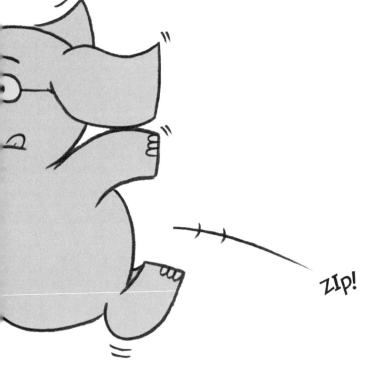

ZIP!

ZAp!

ZAp!

zip!

Is this fancy?

31

32

# What if it is a pool party?

A fancy pool party?

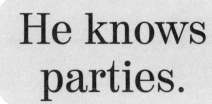

He knows
parties.

ZIp!

ZAP!

ZAP!

zip!

We will make a splash.

45

46

49

51

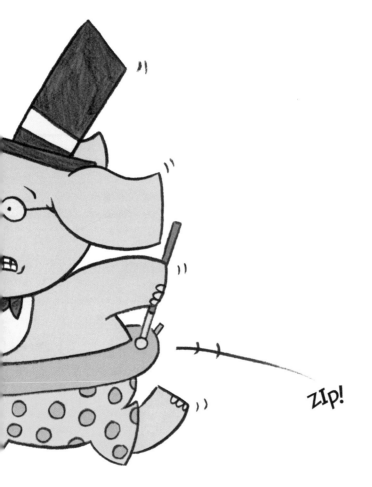

ZIp!

He had better
know parties. . . .

ZAp!

ZAp!

ZIP!

Well, that is a surprise.

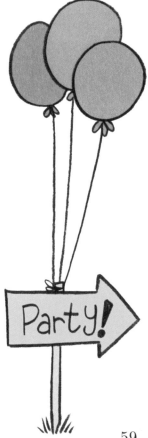

Party!

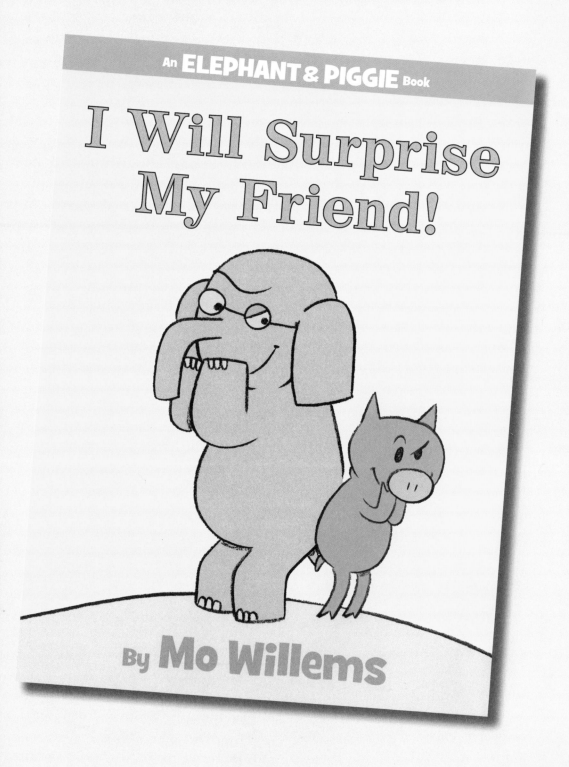

An **ELEPHANT & PIGGIE** Book

# I Will Surprise My Friend!

By **Mo Willems**

Originally published in June 2008.

# I Will Surprise My Friend!

An **ELEPHANT & PIGGIE** Book
By **Mo Willems**

Hyperion Books for Children / *New York*

Hee hee hee!

71

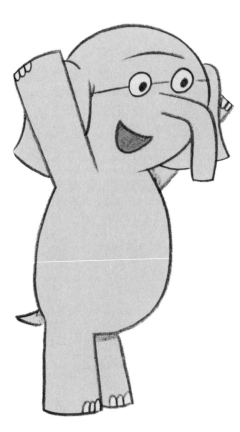

We could surprise each other!

Hee hee hee!

Hee hee hee!

Hee hee hee!

Where is Gerald?

Where is Piggie?

Where can my friend be?

...a giant bird grabbed
Piggie and flew off
with her!

LUNCHTIME!!!

114

That was a surprise.

A big surprise.

121

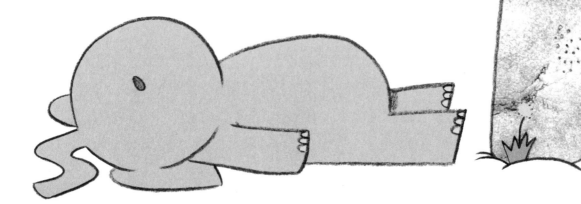

Deal.

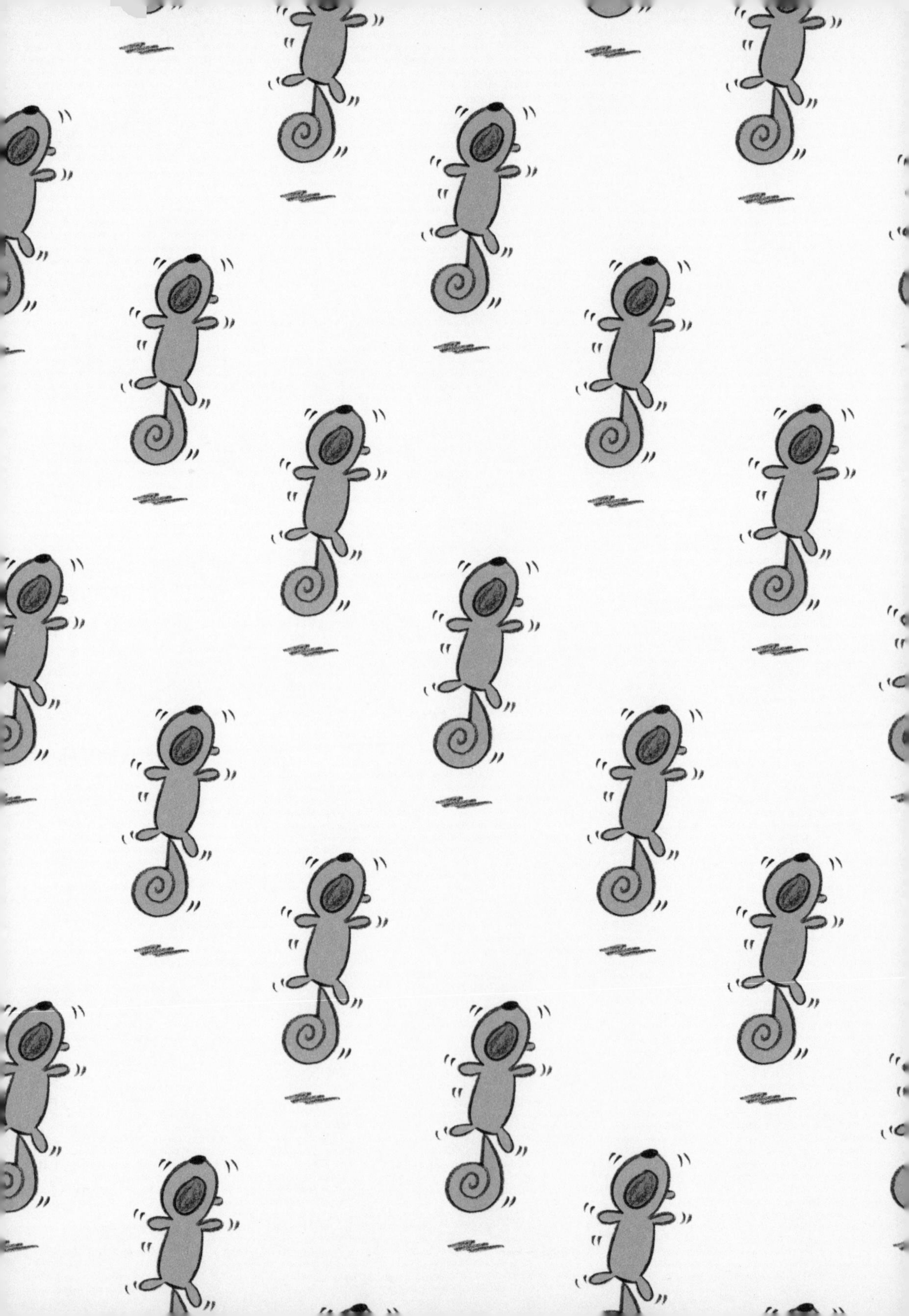

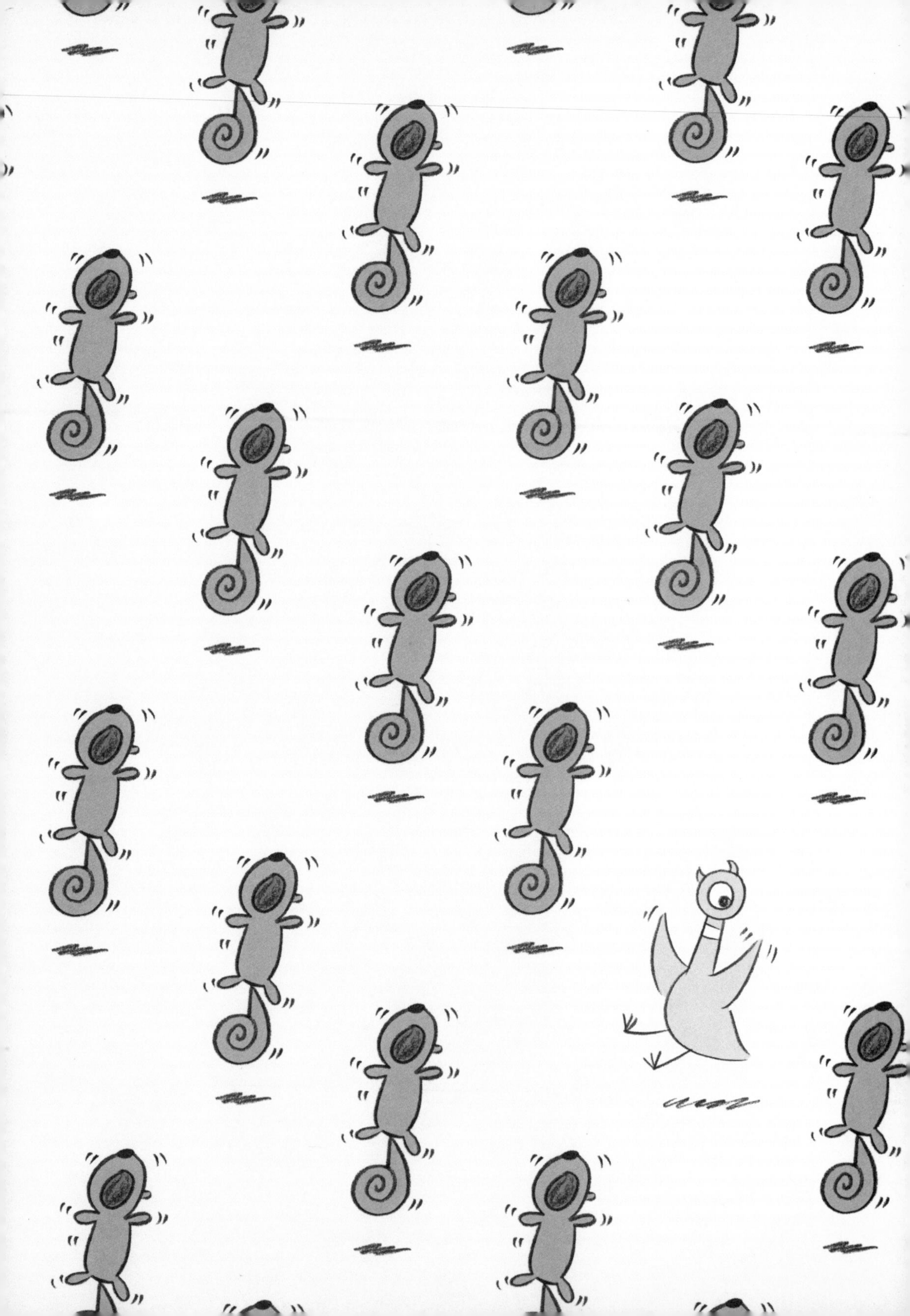

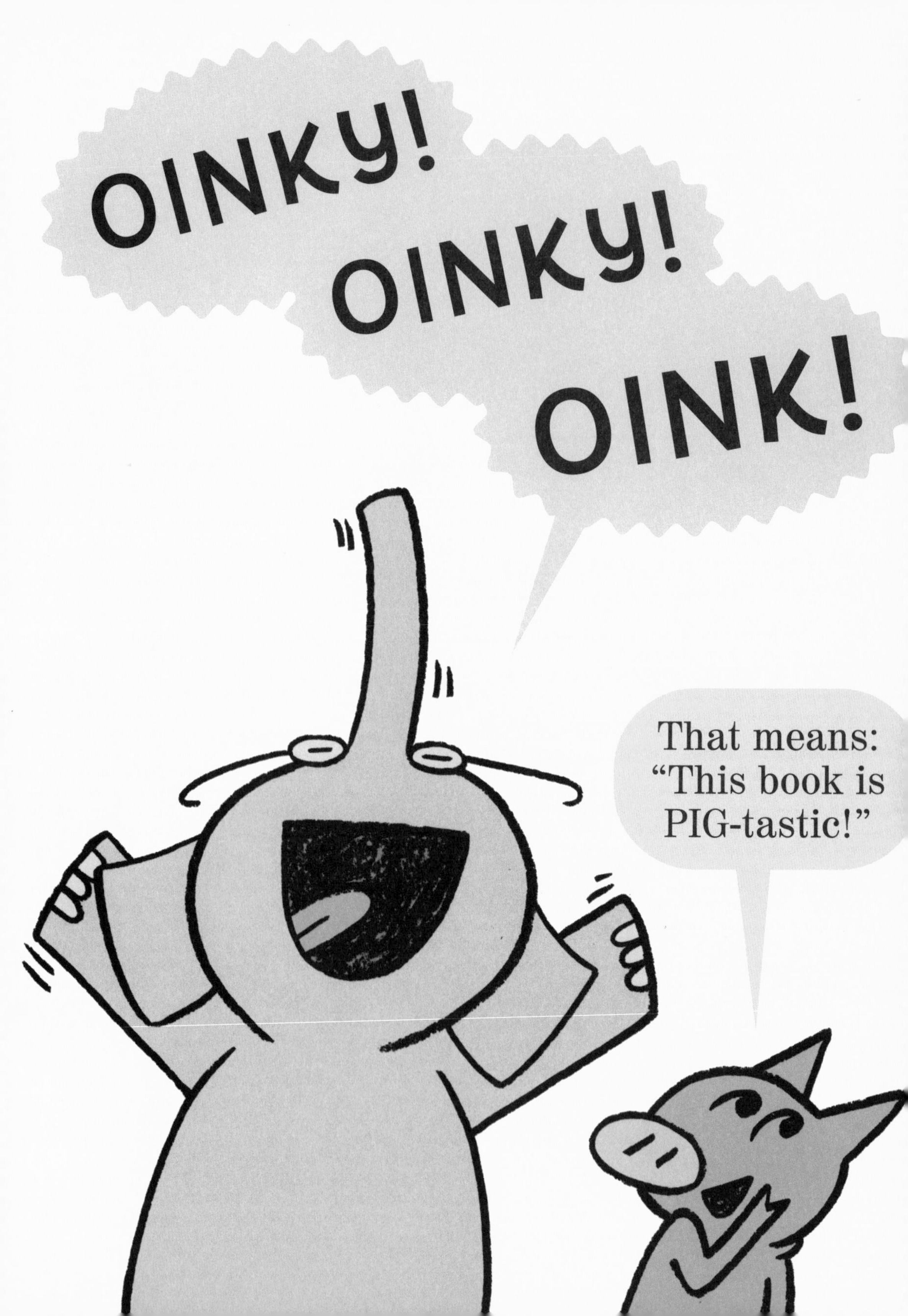
OINKY! OINKY! OINK!
That means: "This book is PIG-tastic!"

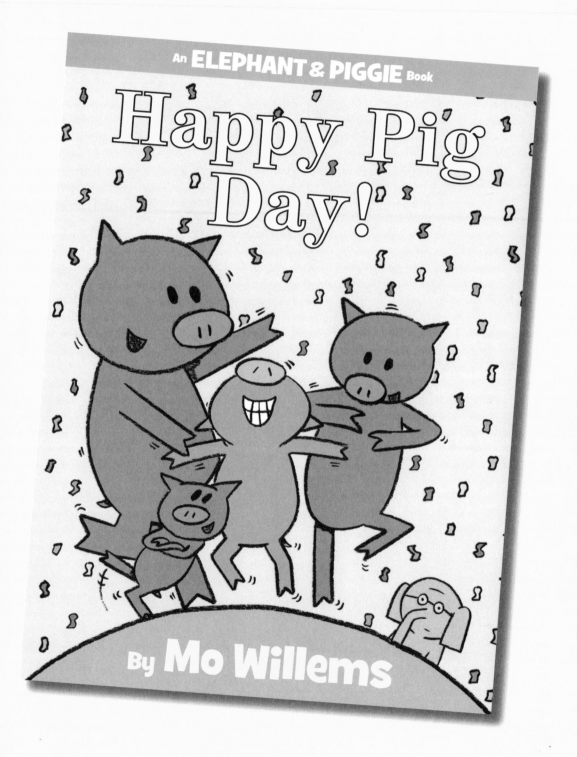

By Mo Willems

Originally published in October 2011.

An **ELEPHANT & PIGGIE** Book

Hyperion Books for Children/*New York*

Gerald!

zIp!

Today is the *best* day of the year!

135

HAPPY PIG DAY!

Happy Pig Day?

It is the best day
to play pig games!

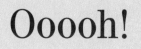

Ooooh!

I did not know about Happy Pig Day.

Look!

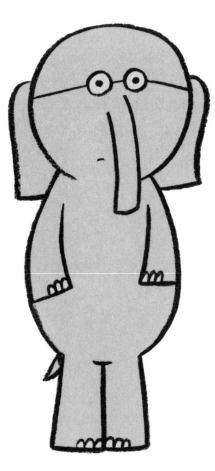

That is a
lot of pigs.

153

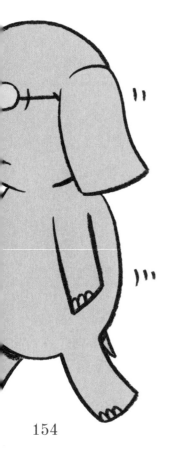

Isn't this great,
Gerald?

157

I do not have hooves!

169

175

# Happy Pig Day is for . . .

179

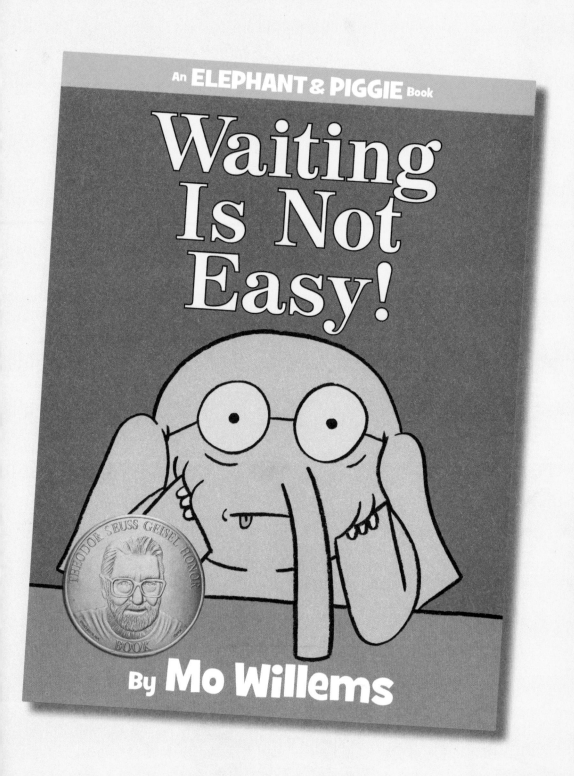

An **ELEPHANT & PIGGIE** Book

# Waiting Is Not Easy!

THEODOR SEUSS GEISEL HONOR BOOK

By **Mo Willems**

Originally published in November 2014.

An ELEPHANT & PIGGIE Book

Hyperion Books for Children
*New York*

# Waiting Is Not Easy!

By **Mo Willems**

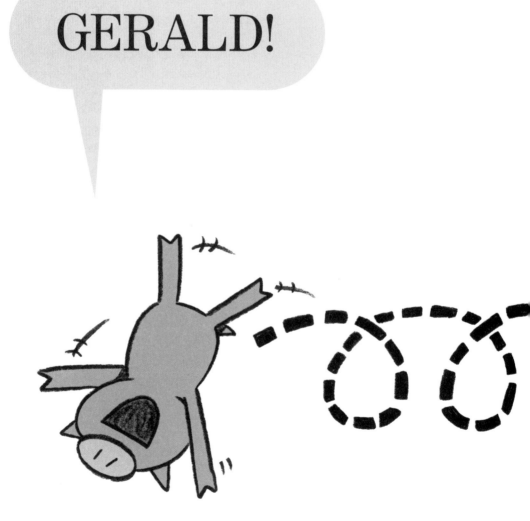

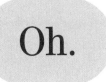

The surprise
is not
here yet.

211

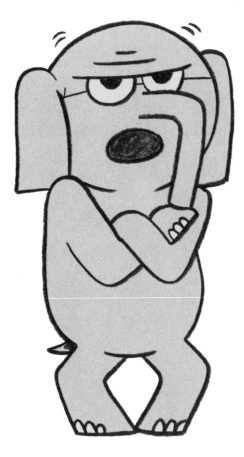

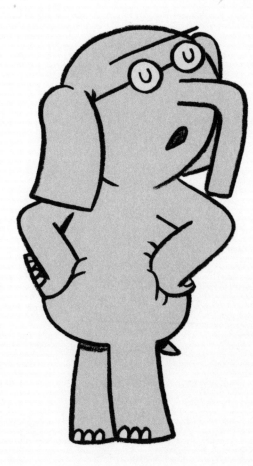

I will not
wait anymore!

Okay. I will wait
some more.

227

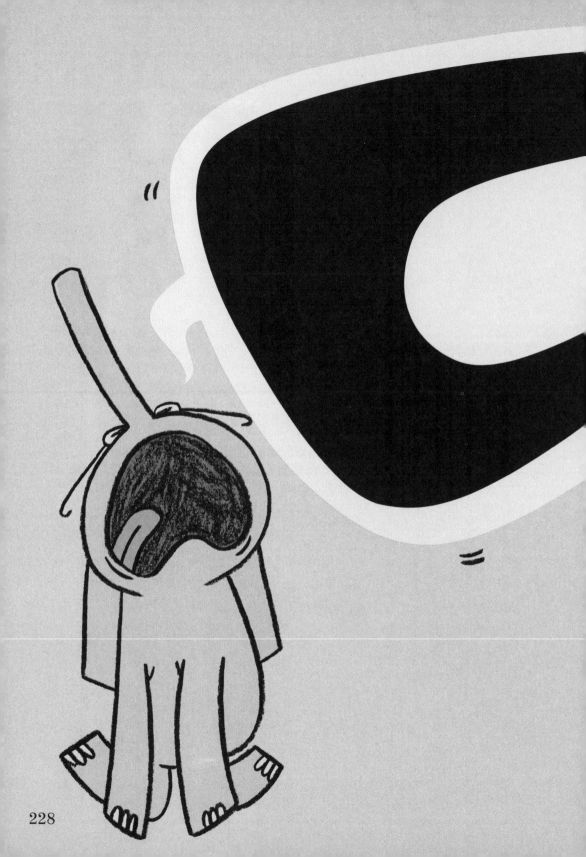

EEK!

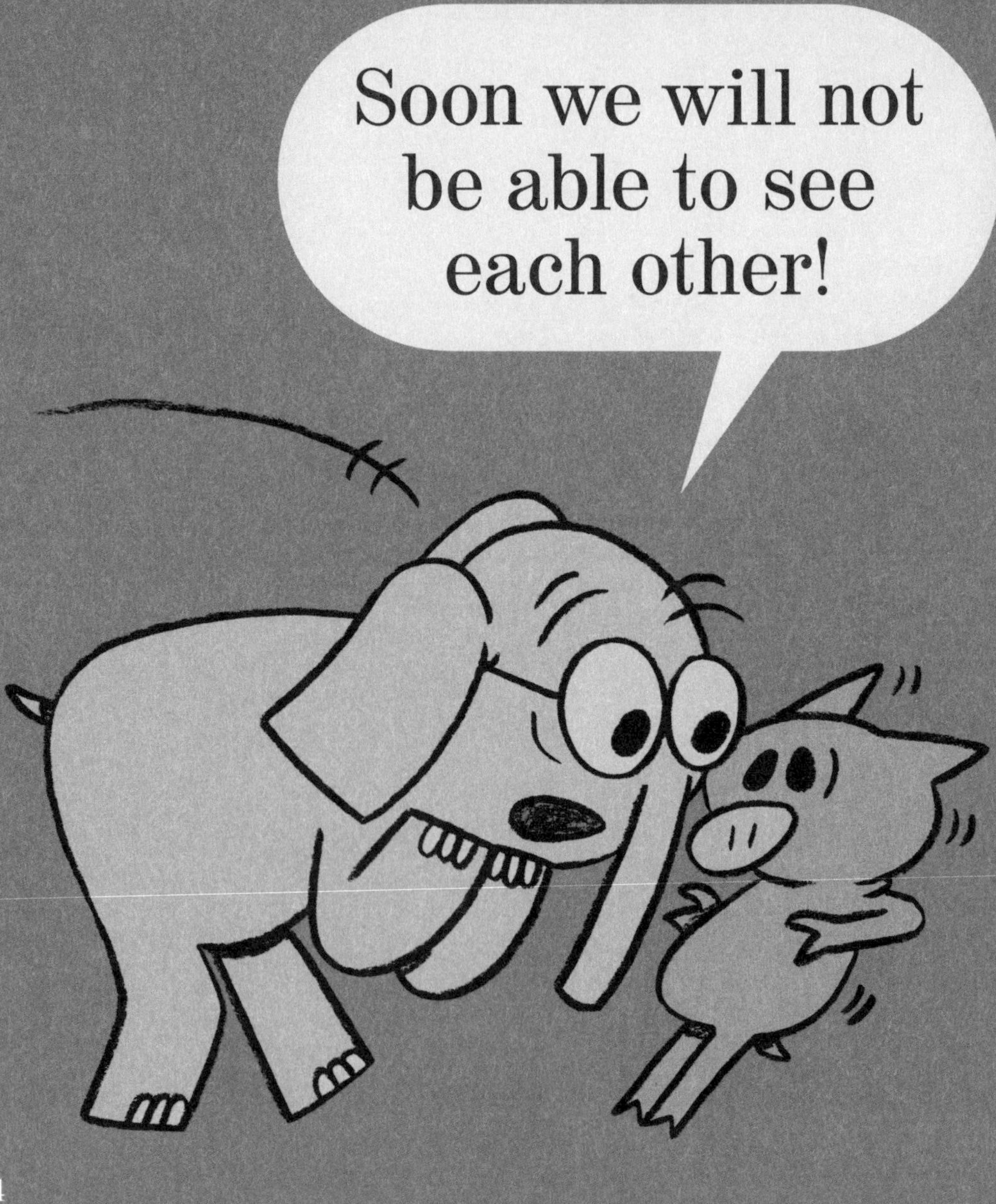
Soon we will not be able to see each other!

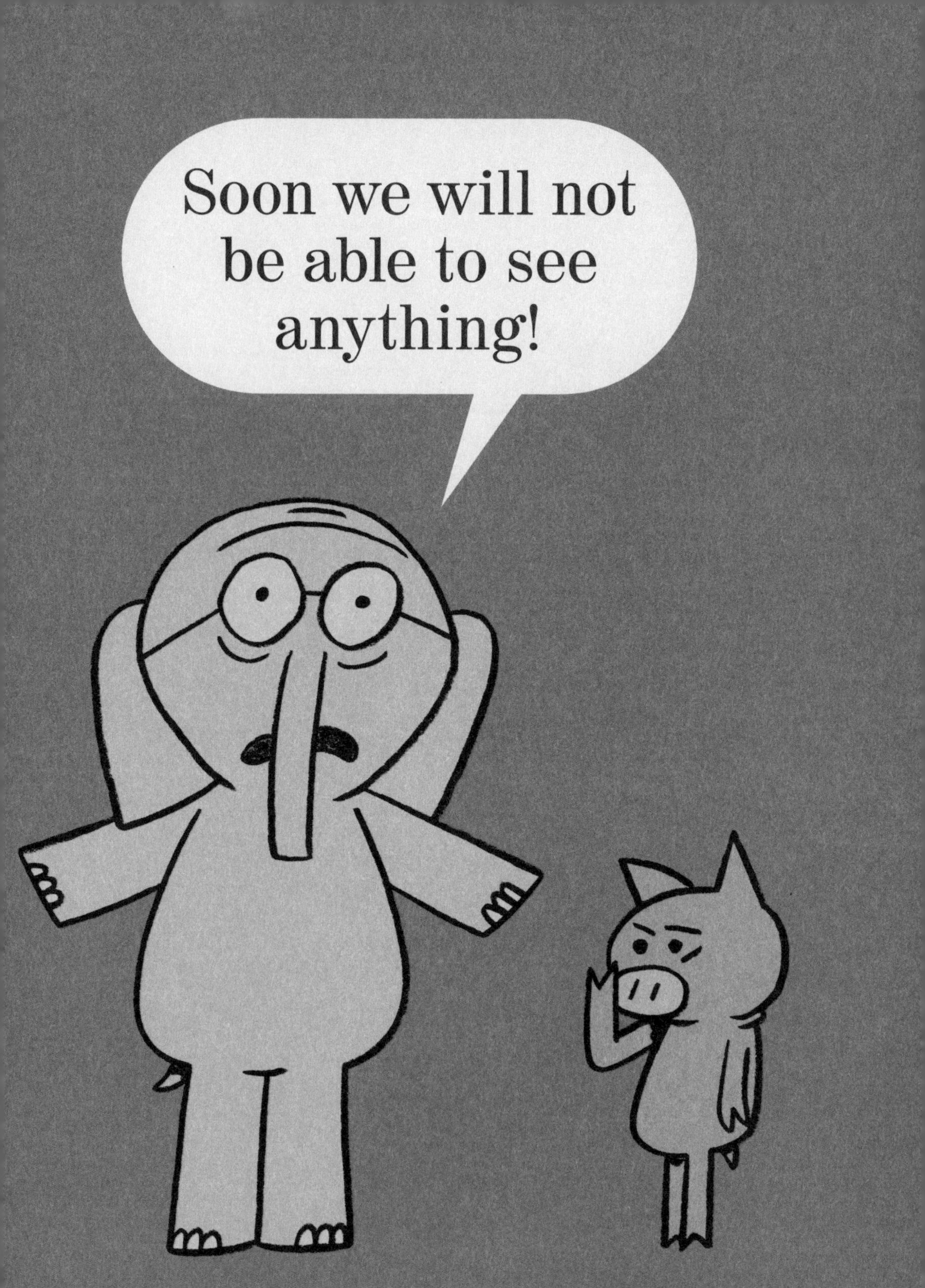
Soon we will not be able to see anything!

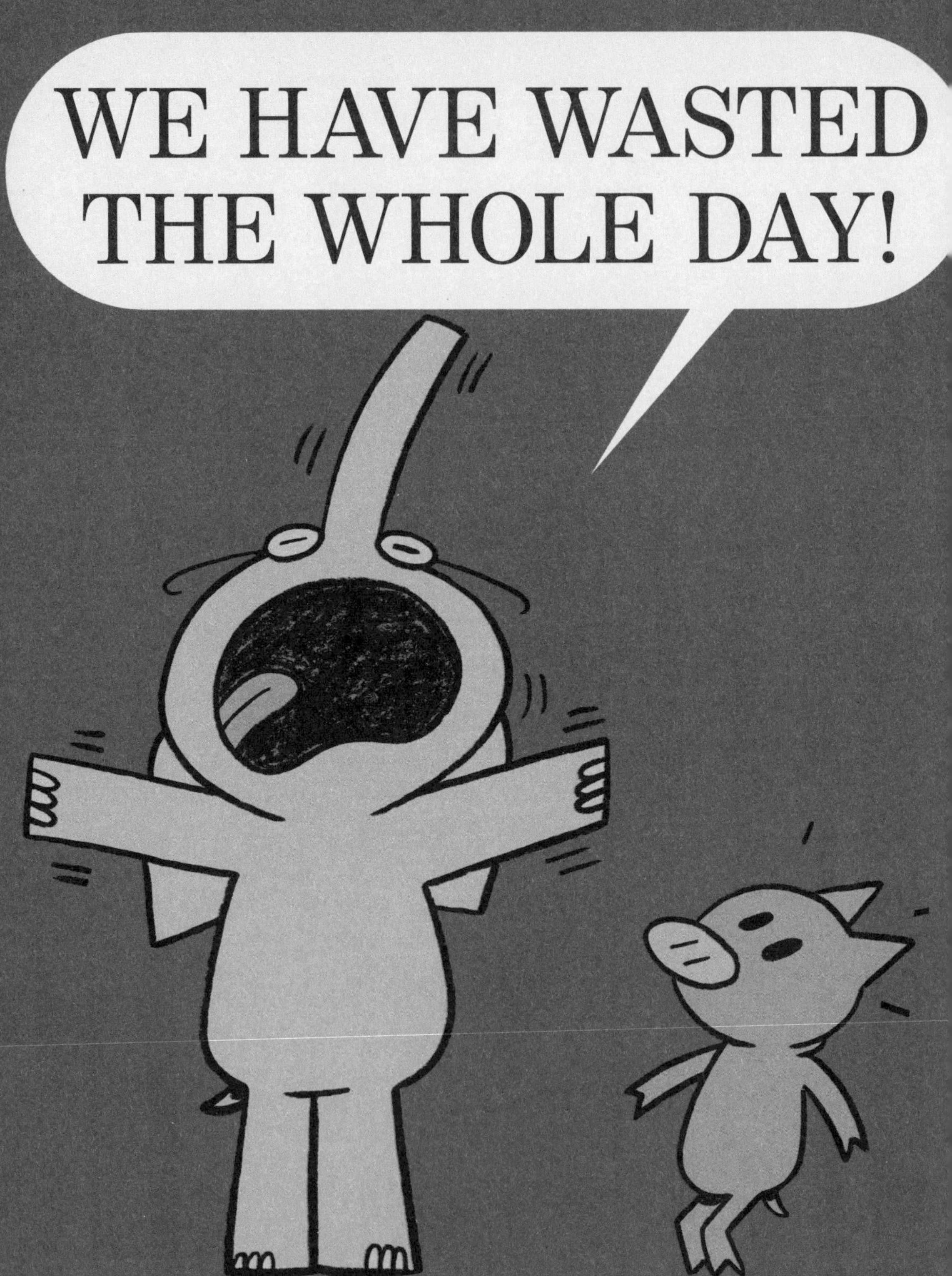
WE HAVE WASTED THE WHOLE DAY!

239

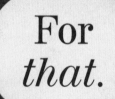

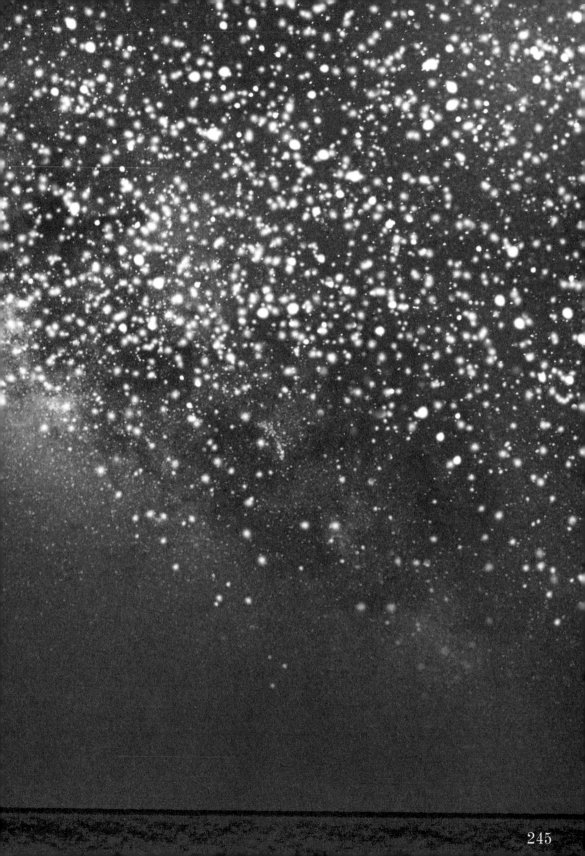

247

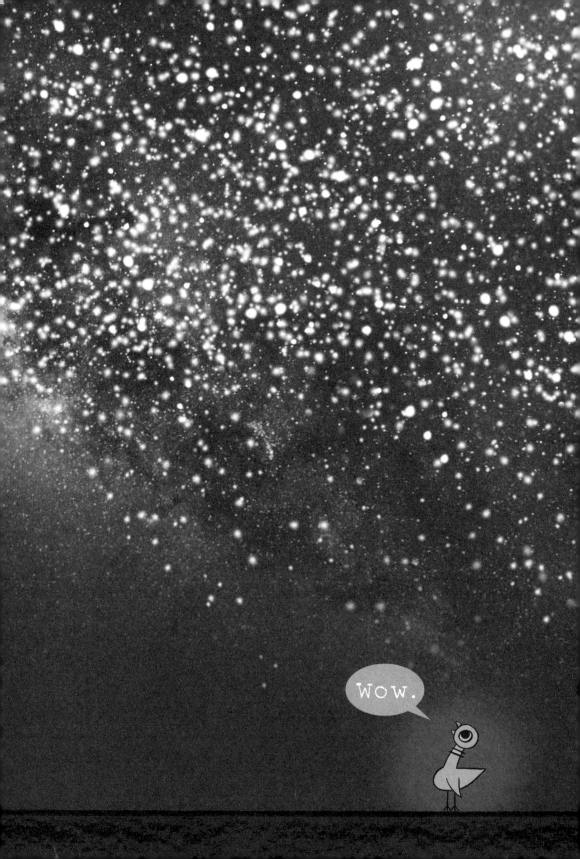

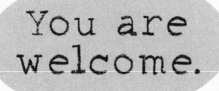

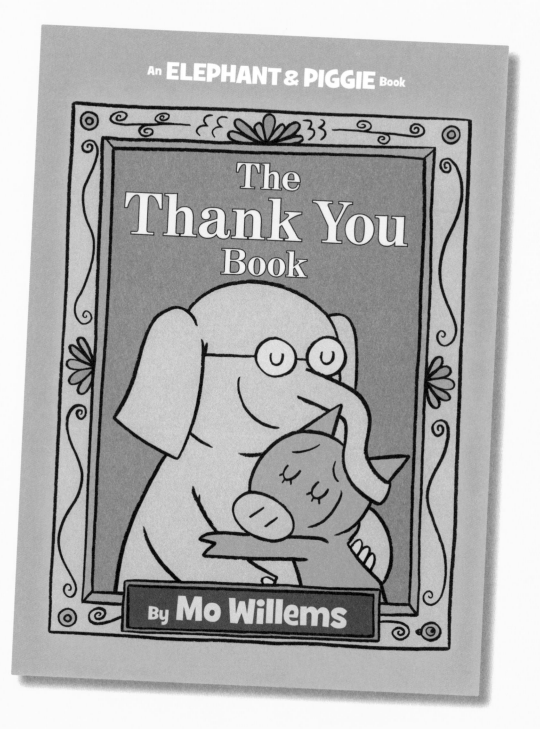

Originally published in May 2016.

An ELEPHANT & PIGGIE Book

Hyperion Books for Children / New York

# The Thank You Book

I am one lucky pig.

By **Mo Willems**

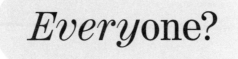

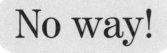

Squirrels!

Piggie!

The Pigeon!

Thank you for never giving up.

Mouse! Birdies! Rhino!
Hippo's Big Sister!
Barky Dog! Pelican! Bear!
Hippo! Worms!

Thank you all for
being great friends!

THANKS, WHALE!

You are nice!

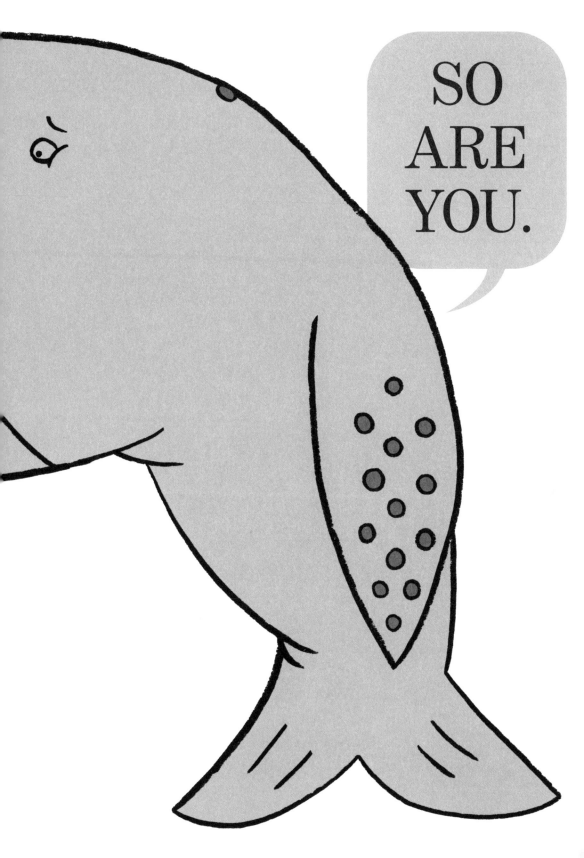

Ice Cream
Penguin!

Thank you
for your
ice cream.

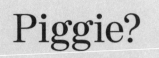

Brian Bat!

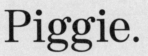

Piggie.

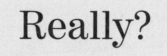

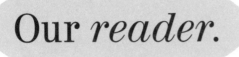

306

307

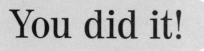

Hippo

Doctor Cat

Bear

The Flies

Hippo's Big Sister

Mouse

Ice Cream Penguin

Snake

Rhino

Brian Bat

Birdies

Worms

Squirrels

Barky Dog

The Pigeon

Pelican

Whale

## Dear Reader,

# Wow!

You read five Elephant & Piggie adventures in one book! Congratulations!

Reading is one of the best ways to celebrate a great day or to turn a not-so-great day into a great day that you can celebrate by reading another book!

When I was a kid, I liked to celebrate by doodling in my notebook, reading Snoopy, and singing super-silly songs. My friend Ryan T. Higgins is celebrating by drawing Elephant and Piggie in his own style. I love it!

How will you celebrate with Elephant and Piggie in your drawing?

Your pal,

**Ryan T. Higgins** has received the E. B. White
Read-Aloud Award and the Ezra Jack Keats New
Illustrator Honor for his *New York Times* best-selling
book *Mother Bruce*. Ryan's other books include
*Norman Didn't Do It!*, *We Don't Eat Our Classmates*,
and *What About Worms!?* an Elephant & Piggie Like
Reading Book!, which received a Theodor Seuss Geisel
Honor. He lives in Maine with his three children, three
dogs, three cats, one gecko, one tortoise, and one wife.